SOZIN'S COMET

CKELODEON

降去神通
AVATAR
THE LAST AIRBENDER.

THE FINAL BATTLE

ADAPTED BY DAVID BERGANTINO
STORY AND POSTER ILLUSTRATIONS
BY PATRICK SPAZIANTE

SIMON SPOTLIGHT/NICKELODEON
NEW YORK   LONDON   TORONTO   SYDNEY

Based on the TV series *Nickelodeon Avatar: The Last Airbender*™ as seen on Nickelodeon®

SIMON SPOTLIGHT

An imprint of Simon & Schuster Children's Publishing Division

1230 Avenue of the Americas, New York, New York 10020

Manufactured in China
3 4 5 6 7 8 9 10
Library of Congress Catalog Card Number 2008922514
ISBN–13: 978–1–4169–5827–7
ISBN–10: 1–4169–5827–4
0211 SCP

Chapter 1
ZUKO

My father must be stopped.

I can't believe it took me so long to realize this. For years I thought only my father could restore my honor. I can't believe I was so naive! Finally, I'm on the right track. Now I'm fighting alongside the Avatar and his friends.

We're hiding out on Ember Island, where my family used to vacation—long ago when we were a family. So that makes it the last place anyone will look for us. Soon the comet will arrive, and Aang has to be ready. I have to help him defeat my father.

⊕ ⊕ ⊕

Aang's training is not going well. He's holding back. His attacks are halfhearted. He can't afford to hold anything back when fighting against my father.

"More ferocious!" I commanded. "Imagine striking through your opponent's heart! Let me hear you roar like a tigerdillo!"

What was that? It sounded more like a PURR than a ROAR. And his flames are so weak that they wouldn't scare a fly! "That sounded pathetic!" I shouted. "I said ROAR!"

"GRRRR!"

Finally! Real flames! We're actually getting somewhere. Aang just needs to keep up the momentum, and we need to keep working. Oh, here's Katara. Why's she bringing him a tray of watermelon juice? He doesn't need refreshments; he needs focus! Great, now the momentum is lost.

This is ridiculous! They're all just lounging around having a beach party, like they have nothing more important to do! They should be helping me motivate Aang, not distracting him and acting like irresponsible kids. He has to face the Fire Lord in three days!

I'll show Aang what it'll feel like to really face the Fire Lord—I'll Firebend a flame so fierce and so hard, he won't know what hit him. . . .

WHOOSH! There! That should remind him what's at stake. . . .

"Get a grip before I blast you off this roof!" he shouted at me.

That's it, come on, get angry!

"Enough!" Aang yelled. BOOM!

Ouch. He just Airbended me through the wall! At least he's getting angry.

"What's wrong with you?" demanded Katara as she and the others caught up with us. "You could have hurt Aang."

I could have hurt Aang? They just don't get it. "What's wrong with ME? What's wrong with all of YOU? How can you sit around all day having beach parties

when Sozin's Comet is only three days away?"

No one has anything to say to that, huh? Why are they all being so weird?

"About Sozin's Comet," Aang said. "I was going to wait to fight the Fire Lord until after it came."

What? How could they not tell me their plans? I thought they trusted me. . . . But I guess I'm keeping something from them too. . . .

"The whole point of fighting the Fire Lord before the comet comes is to stop the Fire Nation from winning the war," Katara announced. "But they pretty much won when they took Ba Sing Se. Things can't get any worse."

I have to tell them what I know—now. I can't believe this. . . . I finally have friends, but as soon as I tell them this, they're going to go back to hating me. . . . "You're wrong. It's about to get worse than you can even imagine. . . .

"The day before the eclipse, I attended a war council. My father had finally accepted me back! He welcomed me in front of everyone and gestured to a seat at his right.

I bowed and took my place. Then General Shinu gave a status report on the occupation of Ba Sing Se. He reported that Earthbender rebellions were frequent and widespread.

"To my surprise, my father turned to me and asked me what I thought we should do. I told him that the people of the Earth Kingdom are proud and strong, and that they can endure anything as long as they have hope. I meant it as a compliment to them. But he took it another way. He vowed that when the comet arrives he will launch a new war over the nations. He said he will burn everything to the ground. He said nothing will survive, that out of the ashes a new world will be born, a world where all the lands are Fire Nation, and he is the supreme ruler!"

There. I said it. I just wish someone would say something, anything. . . . They're all in shock, and I don't blame them. I don't blame them for hating me either. I should have stood up to him. . . .

"What am I going to do?" Aang asked, frightened.

Okay, here's my chance. I have to do my part. "I know you're scared. And I know you're not ready to save the world. But if you don't defeat the Fire Lord before the comet comes, there won't be a world to save anymore."

"Aang," Katara said gently, "you don't have to do this alone."

"Yeah," chimed in Toph. "If we fight the Fire Lord together, we have a shot at taking him down."

"Facing the Fire Lord is going to be the hardest thing we've ever done together," Aang said. "But I wouldn't want to do it any other way!"

Okay, at least he's smiling! Now they're all gathering around him. . . . It's amazing how close they all are. I mean, they are literally willing to do ANYTHING to help one another, while my own sister, my flesh and blood, would plot my destruction without shedding one tear. And now they're all hugging like . . . like family. I guess that's something I'll never experience. . . .

"Get over here, Zuko," Katara called out. "Being part of the group also means being part of group hugs."

Woo-hoo! I mean—I guess I can learn to live with group hugs.

His focus renewed, Aang resumed his training. It's time for me to teach him the most complex and dangerous move yet: redirecting lightning.

"Have you ever redirected lightning before?" Aang asked me.

"Once, against my father." I remember it like it was yesterday. It was just after I told him I was leaving to help the Avatar. He'd already banished me once. This time he meant to kill me. But I turned his lightning back against him and escaped. "You feel so powerful holding that much energy in your body, but you know if you make one wrong move, it's over. Aang, you'll have to take the Fire Lord's life . . . before he takes yours."

In a battle this important, against an enemy as merciless as my father, it's the only way. Everyone else seems to know I'm right, but I know Aang. I think he still thinks there's another way.

But there isn't. I must make him see that.

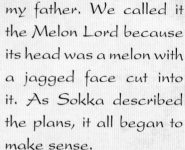

Now that we're all planning to help Aang face the Fire Lord, Sokka created a team training exercise. It seemed ridiculous at first. He set up a crude scarecrow—like replica of my father. We called it the Melon Lord because its head was a melon with a jagged face cut into it. As Sokka described the plans, it all began to make sense.

The exercise itself went like clockwork, but when it was time for Aang to defeat the Melon Lord, he couldn't do it.

This whole thing is so frustrating. I mean, how can WE tell the AVATAR what to do? But at the same time, if he doesn't take our advice, the world will be destroyed! The only way to end this war is to end the Fire Lord's life.

We're gathered for dinner, but no one's really saying much. Then we started talking about the war again. Aang keeps trying to defend his position, saying that the monks taught him the value of human life. As if the rest of us don't understand that? That's EXACTLY what we're trying to do—preserve life! I'm trying to be reasonable with him. I understand that he doesn't want to go around wiping out people's lives just because he's the Avatar and he can. No one would ever ask him to do that! But if he doesn't take my father out, there won't be any life left to preserve. . . . I just can't believe he's being so naive about this.

"No one understands the position I'm in!" Aang yelled.

"Aang, we do understand," replied Katara, "and we're trying to help."

"When you figure out a way for me to beat the Fire Lord without taking his life, I'd love to hear it."

Great, now he's storming out of the room. "Let him go," I told them. "He needs to sort this out on his own."

Aang has a point. This is not a decision to be taken lightly—by any of us. And no one can make this decision for him. He has to come to it on his own.

We all woke up early this morning to prepare for our journey to face the Fire Lord, and Aang is nowhere to be found! We've searched everywhere. His staff is still here, so he can't be far. He'd never leave Appa behind either. We found some tracks leading down the beach and into the sea, so it looks like he went for a walk and kept going when he reached the water. But that doesn't make sense!

"What should we do, Zuko?" Katara asked.

"Why are you all looking at me?" Suddenly I'M the one in charge here? I mean, I guess it's kind of cool that they all trust me and think of me as a leader, but where am I going to lead them?

"Well, you are kind of an expert at tracking Aang," Katara pointed out.

Oh, right. Hey, I know who can help us find him!

I took everyone to the Earth Kingdom to find June, the bounty hunter I had once hired to find Aang, and her Shirshu, Nyla. According to June, Aang is gone — but not dead, whatever that means. It doesn't make any sense, and yet no one, including June, can explain it. We need another plan, and fast. The comet comes in two days! If June and Nyla couldn't find Aang, no one can. And if Aang isn't going to stand up to the Fire Lord, there's only one other person who can: Uncle Iroh. Despite what happened the last time I saw him, I have to go to him. He's our only hope now.

So now June is leading us toward my uncle. I can't believe I'm actually going to see my uncle again. But will he even want to see me? He must hate me after all I've done. I hope he has the heart to forgive me.

"He's beyond the wall," said June suddenly, pointing to one of the ruined walls of Ba Sing Se.

This is it; all that stands between us is that wall. But it's late, and everyone is tired. We'll have to camp here tonight, and wait till the morning to find Uncle Iroh.

⊕ ⊕ ⊕

What's that noise? What time is it? Is it morning yet? Whoa . . . we're surrounded!

"What's going on?" I heard Toph say. "We're surrounded by old people."

Old people? Okay, maybe we won't need to fight. . . .

"Pakku!" I heard Katara shout.

Phew! These people aren't enemies — they're friends. It's a group of great masters. That guy Pakku is Master

Pakku of the Water Tribe. Wow, there sure are a lot of them. . . .

"We're all part of the same ancient society," another master said. "A group that transcends the divisions of the four nations—"

"The Order of the White Lotus!" I cried. Of course! I can't believe I didn't think of it earlier. Uncle Iroh used to talk about it all the time. There were so many things he said that I didn't pay enough attention to. . . . I wish I hadn't been so closed-minded; I would have learned so much more.

"The White Lotus is about philosophy, beauty, and truth," yet another master explained. "But about a month ago a call went out that we were all needed for something important—"

"It came from our Grand Lotus," Pakku interrupted. Uncle.

"Your uncle," he said. "Iroh of the Fire Nation."

Of course he's the Grand Lotus. No wonder those guys in that tavern let us in and hid us. I guess he's pretty important to them. . . .

So we're on our way back to the White Lotus camp. I can hardly concentrate. I'm finally going to see Uncle again, and I can't wait.

Chapter 2
Aang

Yuck, what's that stickiness all over my face? Oh. "Hey, Momo. I had the strangest dream. . . ."

Whoa! Where am I? "Where'd Ember Island go? Momo, where are we?"

This is so weird. Last night I'm asleep on Ember Island, and this morning I'm on some totally strange island in the middle of nowhere! The horizon is empty and everything is gone. Where did everything go? Seems like every time I'm about to face an important battle, I disappear. Usually, I end up in the Spirit World. Hmm . . . I wonder if . . . WHOOSH!

Nope, I'm not in the Spirit World. I can't bend in the Spirit World, and that was a pretty healthy airblast. But this still doesn't feel real to me. What am I going to do?

Okay, just think, Aang. What can you do? I really wish Avatar Roku were here. He always has the answers. Hey wait, I DO have Roku. I'm the Avatar, after all. And I carry around all the past Avatars within me. I just need to meditate and he'll come to me. . . .

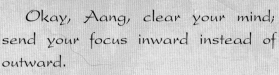

Okay, Aang, clear your mind; send your focus inward instead of outward.

Roku! There you are. "Roku, where is this place?"

"I don't know, Aang, but I see you are lost in more ways than one right now," Roku said.

Roku doesn't even know where I am? This is bad, really bad. I must be truly lost if even he can't help me. But wait, maybe that's exactly it. Maybe until I know how I'm going to face the Fire Lord, this is where I'll stay. Maybe here is where I need to figure that out.

"Everyone expects me to take the Fire Lord's life. But I just don't know if I can do that." Roku has to understand; he's not like everyone else.

"In my life, I tried to be careful and show restraint," Roku said.

See? I knew it. Roku gets it.

"But it backfired when Fire Lord Sozin took advantage of my restraint and mercy. If I had been more decisive and acted sooner, I could have stopped Sozin and stopped the war before it started."

Hey wait, this can't be happening! Is Roku actually apologizing for NOT taking the Fire Lord's life? They were friends! No matter how bad things get, aren't we as Avatars always supposed to show mercy?

"I offer you this wisdom, Aang: You must be decisive!"

13

I'm trying to be decisive, telling everyone that I don't want to kill the Fire Lord. But that doesn't seem good enough for anyone, does it? "Roku, it sounds like you're saying exactly what everyone else is saying. . . . Wait, Roku? Where are you going?"

Okay, so Avatar Roku's wisdom didn't really make me feel any better about things. But maybe he was the wrong Avatar to ask. He seems to think this is all his fault, and maybe that's why he wants me to put an end to Ozai so badly. Maybe I need to ask someone from before Roku's time. Avatar Kyoshi might be more objective.

"Avatar Kyoshi, I need your wisdom."

"Chin the Conqueror threatened to throw the world out of balance. I stopped him, and the world entered a great era of peace."

"But you didn't really kill Chin, technically. He fell to his own doom."

"Personally, I don't see the difference," she said. "But I assure you I would have done whatever it took to stop Chin."

Great! I can't believe this is happening AGAIN! Avatar Kyoshi is saying the same thing as everyone else—that she would have done anything to end Chin's life and save the world. I can't believe it. . . .

"I offer you this wisdom, Aang. Only justice will bring peace."

Humph. Well, I guess that's what I get for asking an ex—Kyoshi warrior.

I really thought that the other Avatars would support my decision, that they would understand what I'm going through. How can these wise and experienced Avatars be so callous?

Maybe I'll do better with the next Avatar. . . . The one before Kyoshi must have been from the Water Tribe. If this Avatar is anything like Katara, I'll find a sympathetic ear. Hopefully Avatar Kuruk can help.

"Aang, when I was young, I was always a 'go with the flow' kind of Avatar. People seemed to work out their own problems, and there was peace and good times in the world. But then I lost the woman I loved to Koh, the face stealer. It was my fault—if I had been more attentive, I could have saved her."

Koh, the face stealer? I remember Koh. I wish I didn't. But that explains Kuruk's sad face. I can't even imagine losing Katara like that! It must have been awful for him.

"Aang, you must actively shape your own destiny, and the destiny of the world." His image shimmers and disappears.

Not Kuruk, too! Again, everyone is telling me the same thing. What am I going to do? Go against everything I know to be true and just?

Wait, just because they were all Avatars doesn't mean they are right. They were as human as I am now, and I've certainly made my share of mistakes. I mean, all of their advice has been based on mistakes they made when they were alive!

Hey, maybe an Air Nomad Avatar will understand me! Okay, Aang, just take some deep breaths and summon the last Air Nomad Avatar. . . .

"I am Avatar Yangchen, young Airbender."

"Avatar Yangchen, the monks always taught me that all life is sacred, even the life of the tiniest spider—fly caught in its own web. I've always tried to solve my problems by being quick or clever, and I've only had to use violence for necessary defense. I've never had to use it to take a life!"

"This isn't about you—it's about the world," she said. Right. That thing I was told to detach myself from so my spirit can be free. Come to think of it, how can an Air Nomad be the Avatar under these circumstances? Now I'm even more confused.

"Many great and wise Air Nomads have detached themselves and achieved spiritual enlightenment," Avatar Yangchen said. "But the Avatar can never do it, because your sole duty is to the world."

Oh boy, even an Air Nomad Avatar is telling me to take Ozai's life.

"Here is my wisdom to you, Aang. Selfless duty calls you to sacrifice your own spiritual needs and do what it takes to protect the world."

She's gone.

"I guess I don't have a choice, Momo. I have to kill the Fire Lord."

Wait, something's happening. A breeze just picked up. . . . The island—it's moving!

Chapter 3
Azula

Normally I love a palanquin ride. It's certainly better than walking like a commoner. And I am no commoner. I am a princess. Princess Azula, to be precise. And I am nothing if not precise. I've found that nothing says "Now THERE goes a princess" like being carried around on the backs of eight strong men. But I wish they would get it over with already. I'm just not in a basking mood today.

I SHOULD be ecstatic! Who in my position wouldn't be? This is the most momentous palanquin ride of my life. My father, Fire Lord Ozai, and I are about to make history together! Side by side, we will burn the Earth Kingdom to the ground. Now that's what I call quality father–daughter time.

I can't wait to get on the airship with Father and leave this place. It's gotten so dull lately. With Zu-Zu off with the Avatar, I have no one to torture. . . . Wait a minute — why am I stopped? And why is my father already walking up the stairs to the giant airship without waiting for me? I better hurry to catch up with him. . . .

Finally! "Sorry I'm late, Father. Good palanquin bearers are so hard to come by these days. Is everything ready for our departure?"

"There has been a change of plans, Azula. I have decided to lead the fleet of airships to Ba Sing Se alone. You will remain here, in the Fire Nation."

WHAT? Him leading the attack? Me alone, left behind? This can't be!

"I thought we were going to do this together!" This is absurd! I've been the perfect daughter. He can't leave me behind. He just can't!

"My decision is final." Oh, no! He really is serious! But I'm the strong one in the family. And I've been unquestioningly loyal. I've proven myself over and over again.

"You—you can't treat me like this. You can't treat me like Zuko!" Why is he doing this to me?

"Azula, silence yourself."

I can barely hear him, I'm so angry and upset. "But it was my idea to burn everything to the ground! I deserve to be by your side!" I'm shaking; I've never raised my voice to my father before— never! Oh, no . . . what will he do to me now?

"Azula!"

Is he going to attack me like he attacked Zuko? I'm better than Zuko, but even I can't beat my father in a duel. It's all I can do to get ahold of myself.

Oh, wait, he's calming down. . . . He's saying that he wants me to stay behind to watch over the Fire Nation, that he trusts me. But something still seems wrong. If he trusts me so much, then why won't he take me with him? Surely he realizes how small watching over a petty little nation is compared to ruling the world. And that's my destiny—out in the world, not trapped in this miserable place with no friends or family. . . . Ugh, I'm so angry I could—

"For your loyalty," Father said, "I've decided to declare you the new Fire Lord."

Fire Lord? Hmm . . . I like the sound of that. Becoming Fire Lord I can understand. So this is what he meant by watching over the Fire Nation. "Fire Lord Azula" does have a nice ring to it. . . . Mai and Ty Lee will really regret betraying me now. And just wait till I catch up with Zuko—hey, wait a minute! There can't be two Fire Lords. . . .

"Fire Lord Ozai is no more," he said.

Now Fire Sages are replacing his cloak and helmet with ones that bear a new symbol: a golden phoenix. Suddenly, that golden phoenix symbol is everywhere, replacing Fire Nation flags all over the palace!

"I am the Phoenix King," he declared.

Now everyone is bowing to him. I guess that's my cue, even if I am the new Fire Lord.

Obviously he's been planning this all along! I guess even as Fire Lord I'm not worthy enough to know! And because he's the Phoenix King, he couldn't care less about the role of Fire Lord, which is why it's no trouble at all for him to toss it to me, as if it were some grand reward. Please! It's charity, and I don't need charity.

And now he's off. . . . So long, Father!

I will show them. I'll show all of them—Zuko, Mai, Ty Lee, and especially Father. They've underestimated me. And they will live to regret it. I WILL be respected. I will rule the Fire Nation. And soon everyone will yield to my power . . . if they know what is good for them.

Chapter 4
Iroh

This morning I awoke thinking of Zuko. It's strange, but I can feel his presence more strongly than usual. I must have been dreaming. But the feeling won't go away. It is as if he is right here with me. But that's impossible! My mind must be playing tricks. I just wish he would find his way back to what is good, to what he is destined to do. I tried to show him, but he must find it on his own; I know that now. His banishment was so difficult for him. He was only a boy when his father attacked him and scarred him for life. When he came to me, I swore that I would take care of him as only a true father could. I hope I did not fail him.

What is that? I hear a voice behind me.

"Uncle, I know you must have mixed feelings about seeing me."

Oh, my! I think my heart will burst from happiness! Fate has returned Zuko to me. And he's apologizing. I knew he would find his way. He always does. But he still does not understand that I will always love him like a son, no

matter how many mistakes he makes. He does not need my forgiveness any more than he needed his father's approval. Still, it's nice to hear. But I suppose I should put him out of his misery and let him know that I accept his apology. A nice, big hug ought to do it. . . .

"I was never angry with you, Zuko. I was sad because I was afraid you had lost your way."

"I did lose my way."

"But you found it again, and you did it by yourself. And I'm so happy you found your way here."

"It wasn't that hard, Uncle. You have a pretty strong scent."

Huh, and I see he's picking up some of my witty sense of humor, too.

Now that we're done with apologies, it's time for food! I certainly could enjoy a nice warm cup of tea. And all of Zuko's new friends are joining us. . . . It's so nice to say that: ZUKO'S FRIENDS! He's always been so lonely, living in that big palace with his awful father and sister; I did not think I would ever see the day when he found a real family of friends who were like him. Ah yes, I remember the young Waterbender, Katara, very well . . . and the Earthbender, Toph. . . .

But apparently, the Avatar is missing. This is very

bad, very bad indeed. They must find him.

"Uncle, you are the only person other than the Avatar who can defeat the Fire Lord."

Oh, dear boy. This is all wrong! "History would see it as more senseless violence, brother killing brother over power. The only way for this war to end peacefully is for the Avatar to defeat the Fire Lord. Then someone new must take the throne—an idealist with a pure heart and unquestionable honor. It has to be you, Prince Zuko."

"Unquestionable honor? But I've made so many mistakes."

Ah, that's my Zuko. He has come so far, but he only sees his mistakes. I wish I could make him see how good he IS, and how bad he could have been.

"Zuko, you have struggled and you have suffered, but you have always followed your own path. You restored your own honor, and only you can restore the honor of the Fire Nation." He looks so proud. Perhaps my words have sunk in. Perhaps he will finally see that it is his destiny to restore our honor and rule the Fire Nation the right way.

🏮 🏮 🏮

There is still much to do to help the Avatar on his journey for peace. I cannot believe how brave these young fighters are. I see the future members of the Order of the White Lotus before me. . . .

Luckily, we "old men" have the easiest job of all: Soon we will free Ba Sing Se. Perhaps that will make up for the horrible sins I committed against the once great city so long ago. And then I will reclaim my tea shop and retire.

Ah, a return to the good life!

Zuko must face something far more dangerous.

"Zuko, you must return to the Fire Nation so that when the Fire Lord falls, you can assume the throne and restore peace and order. But Azula will be there waiting for you. . . ." To reclaim the throne, he must knock her off of it. But Zuko has a heart, and facing her will be difficult, for she is not only powerful, but treacherous as well.

"I can handle Azula."

"Not alone."

"Katara, would you like to help me put Azula in her place?"

Thankfully, he is not so stubborn anymore.

"Zuko, it would be my pleasure!" she said.

Her father must be proud to have such a strong daughter. . . . Hmm . . . I wonder if Katara and Zuko would make a good match? Ah, I suppose now is not the best time to ask. I'll just send him away with these words of wisdom I found on the back of my teabag.

"Today, destiny is our friend. I know it."

Inspiration can be found everywhere, as long as you are looking for it.

Chapter 5
Aang

The island's moving! I'm moving! And it's . . . amazing. From the top of the island's tallest tree, I can see in every direction. And something's moving underwater. What is it?

"It's amazing, Momo—the biggest animal in the world! I've got to swim around and find its face!"

SPLASH! Yuck, the water is really murky and dark; I can't see a thing! Uh–oh, it looks like something's coming right at me. And it's BIG. . . . Phew! Whatever it is, it just missed me. But I better give it some room anyway. . . .

AAAAH! The "thing" was a giant claw! The whole island isn't an island at all—it's some giant creature! This is unbelievable! I have to find this creature's head. It's moving really fast; maybe if I Waterbend I'll get ahead of it. . . . WHOOSH! Made it. This is so incredible. . . . That's an eye! It's kind of strange when I think about it, because this creature is enormous, and yet I'm not even the slightest bit afraid. I know it isn't dangerous. . . . I just wish I knew exactly what it is. . . .

"It's a lion–turtle!" Finally, it shows itself. I have found myself in a lot of really weird places with a lot of weird creatures — that comes with being the Avatar. But I've never seen anything like this. . . . I guess I can say that ending up in odd places is never an accident. It's more like the universe saying, "Hey, Avatar, here are a few more things to think about before you try to save the world." I thought that I was supposed to learn from talking to the past few Avatars, but I definitely don't like what I've heard so far.

So maybe I'm on this island for this lion–turtle — not for the Avatars! Hey, actually, I could have meditated anywhere to speak with past Avatars. Or entered the Spirit World. And this lion–turtle certainly isn't here to eat me! Okay, Aang, just go for it. . . .

"Uh, maybe you can help me. Everyone, even my own past lives, are expecting me to end someone's life. But I don't know if I can do it."

"The true mind can weather all lies and illusions without being lost. The true heart can touch the poison of hatred without being harmed. From beginningless time, darkness thrives in the void, but always yields to purifying light."

Huh. Well, I was right—it can talk. But I'm not quite sure what it means. I don't even know how to reply . . . but even just looking into this creature's eyes makes me feel, well, calm and safe. It looks like it's raising its claw to touch me, and I'm not even flinching. But boy, could that thing do some serious damage! Huh. I suddenly feel less worried about everything. . . .

Whoa, I'm on the ground again, near the shore. I didn't even notice the lion–turtle had lifted me up! And there's Momo! It looks like the lion–turtle is getting ready to leave. . . . But wait, it has something else to say. . . .

"Wait for him. He will come."

Wow. That was truly beyond any other Avatar experience I've had—and look! He took me right to the edge of the Earth Kingdom! The Fire Lord must be nearby. . . .

Look out, Fire Lord Ozai. The Avatar is back!

Chapter 6
Azula

Fire Lord Azula truly has a ring to it. Fire Lord Azula, Fire Lord Azula, Fire Lord Azula. Well, at least one thing can still make me smile. Certainly the dullards around me become less amusing by the moment. Really, they should spend more time repeating the words "Fire Lord Azula" to themselves. Maybe it will inspire them to show the proper respect. Today is my coronation day, after all.

Ouch! These are the worst royal groomers I've ever had! And if the girl with the comb snags my hair one more time, she'll be seeing the inside of a Fire Nation prison within the hour.

Honestly, after my coronation there will be some changes around here. First, I'll—hey! What was that? It was hard as a rock! Who left a pit in these cherries? How very unfortunate for her, whoever she is. . . . Oh, there.

"Do you realize what could have happened if I hadn't sensed the pit in time?" I asked, practically shoving the offending pit into her face.

"You could have choked," the girl squeaked.

She doesn't look clever enough to have left the pit in the cherry on purpose. But it still could have been planted intentionally. Who knows what forces are at work to prevent me from becoming Fire Lord? I need to keep my eyes open from now on. But first I have to deal with this servant. Mistakes — if it was a mistake — will not be tolerated. I should throw this girl in jail. But any lowly guard can throw someone in jail. I'm the Fire Lord. I can do better than that. In fact, I know just what to do!

"You are banished. Leave immediately."

Oh, the look of confusion in her eyes is priceless. Yes, banishing people is a very Fire Lord thing to do. And it passes the time splendidly.

But the cherry pit still bothers me. I'd guess the culprit was Zuko, but he's off with the Avatar. Could Mai or Ty Lee be behind the potentially lethal pit? Come to think of it, these servants are making me suspicious. Sure, they look innocent with their combs and brushes, but in skilled hands any of those seemingly harmless tools could lead to my doom! Time to get rid of them, too.

This day is just crawling by and my hair is still a mess. Seems the only thing that amuses me is banishing people. It comes so naturally!

I ordered the Dai Li to come at once so I could question them, but it took them ages to arrive! So of course I had to banish them all immediately. When the Fire Lord calls you, you come at once! Who do they think they are?

And then there's Lo and Li, my trusted advisors — or so I thought. I can't believe my father sent them to talk to me about all the banishments! I'm the Fire Lord now; I can do whatever I want! He did, and no one questioned him. Besides, if they really were so wise, wouldn't they see all the danger and treachery that surround me here?

Anyway, I'm sure that banishing one of them taught a lesson to the other. I can't tell which one I banished, honestly. In all these years, I never really figured out who was Lo and who was Li. But no matter. They'll figure out which of them is banished, and I'll still have one wise advisor.

Hmm . . . what did that girl with the comb do to my hair? Oh. My. In the mirror. Is that . . . my mother? Is she standing behind me? Well, I won't face her; she doesn't deserve it. Besides, I haven't thought about her for years. She never really liked me. Zuko was her favorite. Who knows what she's doing back here?

"I didn't want to miss my own daughter's coronation," she said.

Oh, right. Like after all this time I'm supposed to believe that she loves me. "Don't pretend to act proud. I know what you really think of me; you think I'm a monster."

"I think you're confused," she said. "All your life you've

used fear to control people. Like your friends Mai and Ty Lee."

"What choice do I have? Fear is the only reliable way." Doesn't she know what they did to me, how they betrayed me? Trust is foolish. If anything, they didn't fear me enough. But they will when I become Fire Lord. "Even you fear me." But I know she doesn't. Now she's looking at me with a pitiful look in her eyes and I can't take it—I feel like screaming!

"No," she said. "I love you, Azula. I do."

Liar! I can't listen to her anymore. I can't! AHH! The mirror, it shattered. . . . There's no one there. My mother, she's gone! Have I been talking to myself the whole time? What's wrong with me?

Finally, the coronation has begun. I was expecting the crowd to be bigger, but apparently, I've banished nearly everyone else. No matter. All that's important is being crowned the Fire Lord. It's time.

"By decree of Phoenix King Ozai, I now crown you . . ." Why is his voice trailing off? Am I going to have to banish him, too? He's not even paying attention to me. For some reason, he's staring into the sky.

Ugh. It's Zu-Zu. And that Waterbender girl. She was the one who prevented me from finishing off the Avatar once and for all. She will pay.

"Sorry, Azula, but you're not gonna become Fire Lord today. I am."

Ha! Now THAT is funny! Now it's time to destroy him once and for all.

"You want to be Fire Lord? Fine, let's settle this. Just you and me, brother; the showdown that's always been meant to be — agni kai!"

Ha! I've got them now. How spectacular! Killing two birds with one lightning bolt. Today is def-initely looking up.

Chapter 7
Sokka

All of these masters and White Lotus members have such great names. I mean, there's nothing wrong with Sokka, but I'd much prefer Master Swordsman Extraordinaire, Boomerang Battle Expert, or, say, the Strategy Guru. . . . I should look into that when we're not busy saving the world from the Fire Lord.

Anyway, Suki, Toph, and I made it from the White Lotus camp to the Fire Nation airfleet base in no time. Which is good, because that's about as much time as we have: none. And still no Aang. But I'm staying positive. The Strategy Guru is staying positive! Huh . . . the name is bound to catch on. . . .

Whoa! There it is! There's Sozin's Comet overhead!

"It's weird to say, but the comet actually looks beautiful," said Suki.

"Too bad the Fire Lord's about to use it to destroy the world," Toph replied.

They're both kind of right, though. It is beautiful, in that signaling-the-end-of-the-world sort of way.

We have to get to the Fire Nation airfleet before it's too late. . . .

We were too late. The airships have already taken off! So it's back to the drawing board. . . .

"Where's the closest airship?" asked Toph.

"It's right—" Aaah! We're flying through the air, going down . . . AH! TOPH!

Phew! We landed! How a blind girl who likes flying even less than riding managed to land us safely on an airship, I'll never know. But we are safe for now. And since we're actually on an airship, my plan might work after all.

Okay. We have to take control of this airship, then we can aim for the Fire Lord's flagship. Hopefully I'll come up with another plan for if and when we catch up with the Fire Lord. As for this airship, I'm thinking a stealthy ruse to—

BAM! Toph's Metalbending armor all around herself. . . . Now she's attacking the captain and crew in the gondola! Phew. That was pretty sweet.

"Good work, Toph. Time to take control of the ship. Take the wheel—"

"That's a great idea, Sokka! Let the blind girl steer a giant airship."

"I was talking to Suki." Nice cover, Sokka. Uh . . . I mean, Master Swordsman Extraordinaire. . . . Good thing she reminded me, though. . . . Why can't I seem to remember that Toph's blind?

I got it! Nothing like a good old-fashioned captain fake-out to steer this airship the right way!

Okay, focus. You're a Fire Nation captain. Go. "Everyone please report to the bomb bay immediately for hotcakes and sweet cream. We have a very special birthday to celebrate."

Ah, the hotcakes-and-sweet-cream trick. Works every time.

And now the whole crew has gone bye-bye through the bomb bay and the airship is ours. Piece of cake! Hey, they really should call me the Strategy Guru. I should look into that. . . . Maybe have some labels made or something.

Time to break formation and head straight for Ozai's ship. Maybe if we just ram into it. No! It's pulling ahead of the main group and gaining speed. We're not going to

catch up with it. Who is that standing on one of the forward platforms? It must be the Fire Lord. He's preparing to Firebend. Oh, no! Fire is raining down from the Fire Lord in a giant fan, scorching the earth below it. So THIS is how the comet boosts the Fire Lord's bending. How can we fight that? How will Aang fight, if he even appears?

Wait, what's that? One minute the Fire Lord is serving up barbecued Earth Kingdom. The next, giant rocks are flying out of the sky, smashing the engines on the Fire Lord's airship! Who's doing that? Wait, is that—YES! It's Aang!

"The Fire Lord is Aang's fight," I told Toph and Suki. "We need to stay focused on stopping that fleet from burning down the Earth Kingdom."

How are we going to take down an entire fleet of Fire Nation airships? Wait, I've got it—

"Airship SLICE!" I shouted.

Wait until those Firebenders see this. I'm such a genius. It is pretty risky, though. We're lucky that no one's noticed we've broken formation. Okay, here goes nothing. . . .

🔶 🔶 🔶

Well, thanks to Master Swordsman Extraordinaire, Boomerang Battle Expert, and the Strategy Guru— a.k.a. ME—we managed to take down the airships and stop the destruction of the Earth Kingdom. . . . It was a little tricky at times, and Toph's Metalbending and Suki's Kyoshi warrior-ness definitely helped. . . .

See, my plan was working until Suki fell off the airship onto another airship, and Toph and I found ourselves on a different airship surrounded by Firebenders!

Dodging the attack, we slid down the side of the airship. I landed on a platform below, but my leg twisted under me. I could barely move. Toph missed the platform entirely, and was holding onto  my hand, dangling hundreds of feet over the Earth!

Suddenly two Firebenders appeared, one on either side of us. With only one free hand and my leg trapped, things did not look good. But we weren't beaten yet. One free arm meant I could throw Boomerang. Boomerang knocked out one Firebender before he got a good blast off. Another swift move and my space sword sliced away the opposite platform, leaving the other Firebender dangling helplessly by a safety rope.

My space sword wasn't so lucky; it fell to Earth. Boomerang didn't come back either. To make matters worse, several more Firebenders appeared at our platform. Then, suddenly, another airship was heading straight for us from below. Its prow cut into the belly of our ship, disabling it. Just as it hit us, I flung Toph and me onto it. Toph couldn't believe our luck. But it wasn't luck. It was Suki. She had commandeered an airship. She saved us!

I'm going to miss my weapons, but I'm just glad everyone is safe and sound. It was a really close call. Now all that's left is for Aang to battle the Fire Lord. . . .

Chapter 8
Phoenix King Ozai

Soon this will all be mine, and everything will be ruled by the Phoenix King . . . just as soon as I get my hands on the Avatar and end the cycle—forever!

Before the Phoenix rises, there must be ashes. Yes, there he is . . . the Avatar. . . .

"After generations of Fire Lords failed to find you, now the universe delivers you to me as an act of providence!"

"Please listen to me; we don't have to fight. You have the power to end it here and stop what you are doing."

Child! Of course I have the power! I've had it all along! "You are right, Avatar, I do have the power. I have all the power in the world!" What a fool! He thinks I'm just going to give up—just like that—because he asks me to? Ha!

WHOOSH! Time to show him some Firebending moves he's never seen! He won't know what hit him, and then I will finally rule. . . .

But he is quick, this Air Nomad. And he keeps deflecting my strikes left and right! But I see fear in his eyes. Oh, he hasn't tasted true fear yet. . . .

I just wish he would hold still. All he does is hop from place to place, avoiding my attacks. Stand still, boy, you can't run forever! You have all the elements at your disposal to use against me, yet you use none in attack. It doesn't make sense! Why does he only seem to defend? I can sense the power in him, but not the instinct to win. Without that, his power means nothing. Clearly he is not at ease with his own powers.

Excellent. It's only a matter of time before he falls. Soon he will tire of bending great columns of stone that never find their marks. His airblasts will be shrugged away by my blasts of fire, and his water attacks will be vaporized instantly. With each failure, he will push himself that much closer to making a crucial mistake. I just have to bide my time. . . .

It's a joke, really. This boy standing before me is the world's only hope? This child who could not save Ba Sing Se from falling? Who failed to take advantage of my one weakness, the eclipse? How could this flawed and insignificant being inspire anyone? I am glad Zuko escaped me that day. He will live

to see that his treachery has amounted to nothing.

Despite his increasing desperation, the Avatar continues to avoid my attacks. But I can tell he's slowing down . . . just a few more steps and FINALLY! I've got him!

Time to unleash my ultimate power: lightning! Just focus all the power of the comet . . . I can feel it . . . a charge far greater than the world has ever known! I can feel the blue electricity crackle. . . . It's time. . . . I will triumph over the Avatar at last—

What's this? What's he doing to it? Why didn't it go through him? He's . . . he's catching the lightning and absorbing it! So my little Zuko has helped the Avatar after all. But the lightning I shot at Zuko was nothing compared to what is coursing through the Avatar now. No one can control that much power—no one!

But still he's not falling. He's fine. What is he doing now? Pointing his hand at me, like he's going to use my own power against me. This is ridiculous! He doesn't have the strength or the training! There is no way this is possible.

Of course! I should have known he wouldn't have the guts to release it on me! Only to send it soaring into the sky. . . . What a weakling! Ha–ha! This weakness will be his downfall, and my good fortune!

Chapter 9
Katara

I can't believe Zuko agreed to this crazy agni-kai thing. Even if it is a tradition, this is not a traditional situation. The entire world is at stake, not just a throne. And Azula is far from a normal person. Zuko is right about one thing, though. Something IS off about her today. She was never likeable. Now she is downright scary. She never seems to stop laughing, and her voice has gotten higher and, I have to say, kind of crazy-sounding.

I just wish I could help him! Any moment now, the battle will begin and I can't do anything about it. To interfere would be inappropriate. It would damage Zuko's honor, and he doesn't need that. Not now. But standing at the side doing nothing is driving me crazy. I am afraid to watch, but I am afraid to leave, too. Azula might be "off," but in a way that just makes her MORE dangerous, not less. Who knows what tricks she will pull?

"Zuko, watch out!" Phew! Azula's intense blue flames just missed him, but Zuko didn't even flinch! I can't believe it's come to this . . . brother and sister, fighting to the end. . . .

I mean, Sokka and I barely argue, and never seriously when we do. I suppose I shouldn't be so surprised. Look at the family I'm talking about! How can they know any better when their father is out to destroy the world?

WHOOSH! Finally! Zuko just knocked Azula off her feet. She's breathing hard now. Zuko's tiring her out, but he looks as fresh as he did at the beginning of the duel. He is going to win and he knows it. And like a brother, he takes the chance to tease his sister.

"No lightning today?" he called across the courtyard. "What's the matter? Afraid I'll redirect it?"

Don't get too cocky, Zuko!

"Oh, I'll show you lightning." She's practically cackling.

I hope he's prepared! She looks fierce, with a wild look in her eyes—Aaah! I can't believe it! She just sent a blast at ME!

Zuko, no! He tried to shield me from the blast. . . .

I can't believe it! He really has changed. . . . But now he's hurt! I have to heal him. . . .

"I would really rather our family physician look after little Zu—Zu, if you don't mind!" Azula shouted.

Oh, no! Zuko isn't moving. . . . I need to get to him, but first I have to take care of Azula! WHOOSH! Take that water blast! Oh boy, she's totally lost it! I can't see anything; blue flames and lightning are coming at me from every angle! Okay, Katara, just stay calm. . . . But she keeps blocking my path to the reflecting pools, and without water there is no way I can defeat her! I have to find a way to fight her. I have to think. . . .

There! At the edge of the plaza. I can hear it: the sound of running water. It's coming from beneath a nearby grate. There's water running underneath the plaza. Here is my chance! But to do what? I don't just need to survive — I need to stop Azula once and for all. Hmm . . . there are some chains hanging from a pillar above the grate. I know what to do.

Luckily, Azula can't seem to think of anything BUT getting me. So luring her into position isn't very difficult. There. She's standing over the grate. She can't even hear the sound of water running over her own crazy laughter. Okay, it's time to face her now. I hope you're ready for a surprise attack, Azula!

WHOOSH! Ha! You weren't expecting that, were you? Take that, crazy! What's the matter? Having trouble getting out of my ice bubble? Now I just need to get her over to the pillar where the chains are. Encased in ice, Azula is powerless. Good thing, too. Azula's fingers are frozen just inches from my nose! Lightning at that range would have more than just stung!

Okay, time to melt the ice around the chains. Unbelievable! She actually looks scared. . . . Maybe

she finally knows that she's trapped and helpless. . . .
There! The chains are locked around her. She's finally
defeated! Now I just have to attach the chain to the stone
pillar . . . and done. I guess it's time to set her free from the
ice bubble. . . . That's it. Azula is finished!

Okay, time to heal Zuko, finally. Zuko must have been
badly injured with that much lightning flowing through him.
Come on, Zuko, wake up. . . . Oh, he's opening his eyes!
It's working!

"Thank you, Katara."

"I think I'm the one who should be thanking you,
Zuko."

Chapter 10
Aang

I'm falling!

   I showed Ozai mercy and he attacked me anyway— way. If I don't Waterbend a cushion in that lake below me, I'm done for. But maybe I'm done for anyway. . . . I mean, it looks like one of us will have to go down, and I obviously can't convince him to surrender. But I won't kill him. I won't. But if I won't, how will I defeat him?

   Ozai's right behind me. I need some time to think. I'll just create a sphere around me, stall a bit.

   "Come on out, little boy!" Ozai is taunting me, but I don't care. I need to figure this out . . . NOW. . . .

   BOOM! I think that was his most powerful Firebending attack yet. . . . He's getting angry; my stone sphere is getting really hot. The air is suddenly thick and hard to breathe. . . . Come on, Aang, if you don't stay focused, you'll lose, and the world will be in severe danger. . . . Am I just being too stubborn? Maybe everyone is right. Maybe I have to take his life for the greater good. Have I realized what I must do too late? There's no air in here. I can't . . . breathe . . . any . . . more . . .

What? Who's that? Is that . . . Katara? Her face is so clear in my mind—as if she's standing in front of me! If I lose, if I give up, I'll never see her again. I've sacrificed everything, even my ability to enter the Avatar state, for her. It can't all be for nothing. Yes, I have a duty to the world. But I love Katara.

I remember the first time I saw her face. She had rescued me and Appa from the iceberg where we'd been trapped for a hundred years. No! The scene is fading! I don't want to leave that time. . . . Hey, there's Avatar Roku! And the Air Nomads! Everything is happening so quickly. . . . There are all the other Avatars of my past lives. . . .

This feels a lot like my chakra training. But there was so much pain when my final chakra closed to me. This feels different. Hey, I think my final chakra is opening at last! I'm coming back. I've never felt THIS kind of power before. . . . That's it! I'm back in the Avatar state again, for the first time since fighting Azula in Ba Sing Se! But it feels different from before. Usually the Avatar state scares me, and it's hard to control. But this time it's different! I'm in control, I can feel it! Finally! I've become a true Avatar! Suddenly I don't feel like I'm doing this alone at all. . . . I can feel all the other Avatars with me, inside me. . . .

Ozai keeps trying to break my protective sphere. I can barely feel the heat anymore, my power has grown so great. He's teasing me now, as if I'm a little child. I guess it's time to show him what I've become— what WE'VE become. Time to show him who he's dealing with!

Rising into the air, I gather the four elements around me: air, water, earth, and fire. They're orbiting me in perfect harmony and in awesome power. This is an incredible feeling. I can do anything. And the Fire Lord is nothing. He will now be punished for his crimes. WHOOSH!

Look at him, scrambling to his feet, still reeling from my surprise blow.

Okay, he's coming to and resuming his attacks, pitiful as they now seem. . . . He's becoming sloppy and aiming poorly. . . . He's losing it!

Earthbending, I've surrounded the Fire Lord with sheer stone walls, trapping him. He's flinging himself at me, trying to launch one last attack. It's over, Ozai! A small blast lays him out stunned on the ground below. Quick! Entrap his hands before he can move again—got 'em! That's it . . . I have him. . . .

Floating above him, encased in the sphere of the four

elements, the voices of all the Avatars speak through me.

"Fire Lord Ozai," we said. "You and your forefathers have devastated the balance of this world. And now you will pay the ultimate price!"

We're ready to deliver the final blow. . . . ready to strike. . . . This is it. . . . Wait! What am I saying? No, I can't end it this way, this isn't right. What's that— that voice? It's the lion-turtle! Yes, I remember! To bend another's energy, my own spirit must be unbendable. . . . I can do this; WE can do this. . . . That's right, I remember now! I know what to do. . . . I know how to end it!

Time for the other Avatars to go back to where they belong: the past. I won't need them for this. I don't need the Avatar state. I only need myself . . . Aang, alone.

It's just him and me, one against the other. I can't believe I came so close to betraying myself. . . . If all the power in the world can't end this war peacefully, then all the power in the world isn't enough power.

"No. I'm not going to end it like this," I said, turning my back to him.

Sensing my hesitation, Ozai's defiance returns.

"Even with all the power in the world, you are still weak!" he growled. Breaking from his bonds, he attacks.

BOOM! My Earthbending sends him back into his shackles.

Ozai is wrong. They are all wrong. There is no strength in the ability to destroy. Staying true to yourself is a far greater strength, no matter the circumstances. I will defeat the Fire Lord, but I will do it my way. And I finally know how.

He is helpless now . . . it's time. Okay, with one hand over his heart, the other on his forehead, just concentrate and this will work. I know it will! It's just like the lion–turtle said, my spirit has to be unbendable for this to work. I can feel a connection between myself and Ozai's heart and mind, linking them! A new and wild energy

is flowing through me. The lion–turtle also told me that before the era of the Avatar, we bent not the elements, but the energy within ourselves. . . . If I can bend the energy in Ozai, I can stop him from harming ever again. . . .

I finally know what the lion–turtle meant! Little by little,

I'm gaining control over Ozai. It's working! Just find the source of his energy. Once I do that, he will be at my mercy! Finally I can feel it! The lion—turtle was right. This is a new kind of bending, more powerful than control of any given element.

Suddenly there's a blinding flash of white light—it's the purifying light the lion—turtle had spoken of. Boy, does bending someone's life force take a lot out of you! I can barely stand.

"Wh—what did you do to me?" he asked.

"I took away your Firebending," I told him. "You can't use it to hurt or threaten anyone else ever again."

I can't believe it—I actually did it! I defeated the Fire Lord without taking his life! We're safe, we're all safe!

🀆 🀆 🀆

This is by far the best day ever! Toph, Sokka, and Suki are safe and sound, and we're all on our way back to the Fire Nation to find Katara and Zuko. As we traveled, they caught me up on everything that happened since I last saw them. I can't believe we actually did it! Most of all, I am proud. They never gave up hope—not once! Even

when they didn't understand me, they stood by me and supported me every step of the way. And even when I disappeared and they didn't know where I went, they kept going. They kept fighting to save the world. It's truly amazing. . . .

Finally, we're here! I can't wait to see Katara! The palace courtyard is in ruins. . . . Wow, they really tore this place to pieces! Look, there they are!

Phew, sounds like their battle with Azula was pretty fierce. Thank goodness for Zuko. I can't even begin to think about what would have happened to Katara if he hadn't saved her! I could hug him for saving Katara's life. But Zuko's not exactly the huggy type, so I'll save him the embarrassment. To think we were mortal enemies not long ago. . . .

☯ ☯ ☯

Speaking of healing, it's time for Zuko's coronation! It's a grand ceremony. The entire palace is filled with all sorts of friends, family, and even former enemies. It's an amazing sight. Oh, and Katara and Sokka are reunited with their father again, finally! It's so wonderful to see them so happy. Seeing Toph and her Earth Rumble Six rivals, Hippo and the Boulder, acting chummy is a bit weird. But Ty Lee joining the Kyoshi warriors? That's downright surreal.

In a way, I'm happiest of all for Zuko. He is the new Fire Lord. And it seems that he's found a real

soul mate in Mai. She's so much prettier now that she smiles. Best of all for Zuko, even his uncle Iroh is here. He told us how the White Lotus Society had liberated Ba Sing Se and freed the Earth Kingdom. Finally, the Earth Kingdom is free again!

When Fire Lord Zuko—that sounds so weird—announced the end of the war, the crowd's cheering became almost deafening.

"I promised my uncle that I would restore the honor of the Fire Nation," he said. "And I will. The road ahead of us is challenging. A hundred years of fighting has left the world scarred and divided. But with the Avatar's help, we can get it back on the right path, and begin a new era of love and peace."

How strange to hear words like that coming from Zuko! But I'm certainly not complaining. Together, we WILL heal the world.

✦ ✦ ✦

The world has come a long way in the months since the end of the war. With Zuko's efforts, the healing has begun. Of course, being the Avatar, I hope I'm helping at least a little! Best of all, we finally get to relax. Uncle Iroh, true to his word, has reopened his tea shop, the Jasmine Dragon. We gather there when we can. It's nice not to be preparing for a fight. And luckily, with a group of friends like this, things are never boring. Right now they are all bickering over a group portrait that Sokka painted. He means well, but his artistic skills aren't the best. He makes a far better sword master than artist.

I decided to step out of the tea shop for a little Aang

time. I got so lost in my thoughts, I almost didn't notice Katara following me out to the porch!

Hmm. . . . She's just standing there quietly. She must have SOMETHING to say. Why else would she have followed me out here? Gosh, she really is beautiful. It's strange, but it feels like it did in the Cave of Two Lovers, right before the lights went on. Next thing I know, she's hugging me! Cool. And this is going much more smoothly than it did in the Cave of Two Lovers. I guess that's because this time I'm keeping my mouth shut! Oh boy, I can't believe this is happening . . . she's leaning in . . . she's . . . she's kissing me!

This is by far the best day of my life—since I defeated the evil ex-Fire Lord, of course!

Interview with Michael Dante DiMartino and Bryan Konietzko, Creators of Avatar: The Last Airbender

Complete with exclusive, early AVATAR concept sketches from the creators' secret vault!

In rich shows like AVATAR, characters can take on a life of their own beyond what was originally planned or envisioned for them. Did this happen with any of the characters in particular during the course of writing the show?

MIKE: Believe it or not, Bryan and I originally imagined Toph as a muscular, tough–talking, teenage boy. During the development process, we decided that Aang would need an Earthbending teacher and always planned to add this new character to the group in season two. It was our head writer, Aaron Ehasz, who suggested making Toph a girl. We were so used to thinking of Toph as a muscular teenage boy, the idea took some getting used to. But once we applied those same characteristics to a cute twelve–year–old girl, it made the character much funnier and more relatable. Now, Toph is one of our favorite characters, and we couldn't imagine her any other way!

There were several allusions to Katara being Zuko's girlfriend throughout season three. Aside

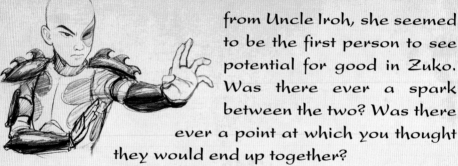

from Uncle Iroh, she seemed to be the first person to see potential for good in Zuko. Was there ever a spark between the two? Was there ever a point at which you thought they would end up together?

MIKE: Sorry to disappoint the "Zutara" fans out there, but we never intended for Zuko and Katara to get together. Maybe we're just sentimental, but we always had a soft spot in our hearts for "Kataang."

BRYAN: Zuko and Katara might have shared some sparks, but sometimes there are people along your "journey of love" who are there to teach you about yourself and what you really need, but don't necessarily end up being your partner. Come on, kids! "Zutara" never would have lasted! It was just dark and intriguing.

When Aang was on the "mysterious island," Nyla could not locate him, and June concluded he wasn't dead but that he didn't exist. That was a head-scratcher! Can you describe how existence on that "island" was different from either reality or the Spirit World?

MIKE: The answer is actually pretty simple. The lion-turtle exists in the reality of the Avatar World, not the Spirit World. But the lion-turtle is thousands of years old, so his ancient, powerful odor masks the scent of anyone on his back. And that's why Nyla couldn't smell Aang.

BRYAN: Yeah, the lion–turtle's scent is so ancient and pervasive that Nyla just perceives it as the smell of the earth itself.

What are each of your favorite episodes over the course of the series, and why?

MIKE: My favorite episodes are the epic ones that really move the overall story forward, like "Siege of the North," "Crossroads of Destiny," "Day of Black Sun," and "Sozin's Comet." But because we have sixty–one episodes in which to tell the story, it's fun to digress from the main plot once in a while and explore other aspects of the characters and their world. Some people call them filler, but I love humorous/romantic episodes like "The Fortune–Teller," "The Cave of Two Lovers," and "The Ember Island Players."

BRYAN: My favorite scenes are when there is a cinematic level of drama present, which can be difficult on an animated TV show. As for favorite complete episodes, I personally love "The Blue Spirit," "The Blind Bandit," and "City of Walls and Secrets."

Katara is an amazing female character, and across the board, good or evil, the female characters

in AVATAR are extremely strong, distinct, and complexly developed. Was this an integral part of your vision, or did you just find that you were good at writing female characters?

MIKE: We set out from the start to make sure the female characters were strong and complex. Even though we were making an action/adventure show, we believed from the start that if there were strong female characters and relationship issues, that girls would want to watch too. We were at a signing once and we asked a male fan who his favorite character was. He was a tough-looking teenager, so I assumed Zuko or Sokka. But I was totally wrong. His favorite was Toph. If a character has strong motivations, a compelling personality, and personality flaws, it makes them very relatable to an audience, boy or girl.

BRYAN: Maybe it is because I have three older sisters, and Mike has a younger one!

Most of the animals in the show are hybrids, like tigerdillos or badger-moles. In fact, the gang not being able to get their minds around the idea that Bosco was simply a bear was very funny. What are the rules for animals on the show, and where

did that hybrid idea come from?

BRYAN: Drawing hybrid animals was a favorite hobby of mine when I was a kid, so when I opened up my imagination to come up with a show with Mike, the manatee—bison creatures just came out. I didn't even think about it, I was just back in a state of my free-spirited kid imagination. Next was a polar bear—Labrador retriever, but sadly he never made it into the show.

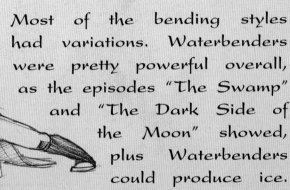

Most of the bending styles had variations. Waterbenders were pretty powerful overall, as the episodes "The Swamp" and "The Dark Side of the Moon" showed, plus Waterbenders could produce ice. Earthbending had sand and metal variations. Fire had lightning. Airbending seemed like a more singular style. Was this intentional, or are there variations we didn't get to see?

BRYAN: I would actually say Airbending is the most versatile of the four, the main difference being Airbenders do not usually use their skills in such an aggressive manner.

Why did Sokka have to lose his space sword AND Boomerang at the end? They were so much a part of his character and his skill set, especially since he lacked bending skills.

MIKE: That's why that scene is so great! These are just two ordinary objects, but over the course of the series Sokka (and the audience) have formed an emotional connection to them. So when he loses them in order to save Toph, it really feels like a sacrifice. And in an epic finale, it's always more satisfying when the characters have to sacrifice something in order to achieve their goals.

BRYAN: Yeah, I would rather be alive and save my friend than have a sword and a boomerang!

Peace has been restored, but if Aang is still the only Air Nomad left, is the world still out of balance?

MIKE: Yes, the world is still out of balance. But just because Aang is the last Airbender,

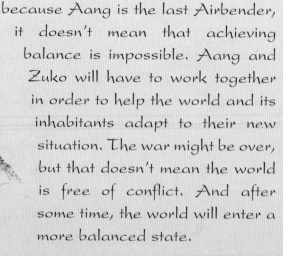

it doesn't mean that achieving balance is impossible. Aang and Zuko will have to work together in order to help the world and its inhabitants adapt to their new situation. The war might be over, but that doesn't mean the world is free of conflict. And after some time, the world will enter a more balanced state.

Can the Air Nomads make a comeback, and how?
MIKE: As the title says, Aang is "The Last Airbender."
It's not likely the Air Nomads will be coming back.

If Aang and Katara had a child, would it be an Airbender, a Waterbender, or a combination-bender? Or would it have limited command of all four elements because Aang was the Avatar?
MIKE: First of all, Aang and Katara are a little too young to be having kids! But if they decide later in their lives that they would like to start a family, their kids could be born a Waterbender, an Airbender, or a non-bender. But they definitely would not have the ability to command all four. Only the Avatar can control all four elements.

Given the richness of AVATAR and the detail-oriented fan base, do you have any plans to create a definitive guide of the Avatar universe?
MIKE: Not right now. Plus, the fan sites are doing a great job of tracking the Avatar universe — they are much more organized than we are!
BRYAN: We have talked about making a book of the art and animation work behind the show, sort of like the Japanese animation "groundwork" books. The main issue is finding the time to do this!

Fans of AVATAR are very enthusiastic and passionate. The Internet is full of fan sites and blogs. Have you ever gotten any ideas about turns for the show from listening or reading what fans are saying?

MIKE: We really appreciate all our fans and their enthusiasm for the show. I occasionally check the message boards to see how the fans receive a particular episode. It's fun to read some of the speculation, but we don't use any of the ideas. From the beginning we've had a very specific plan of how the story would play out.

If you were benders, what kind would you be?

MIKE: I would probably be an Airbender. It would be fun to fly on a glider and have my very own Appa!

BRYAN: I would definitely be a Tarbender.

Of all the characters in AVATAR, who do you think is the strongest, and why?

MIKE: They all are really strong, physically and spiritually. But if I have to pick, I'd say Zuko, because he had the longest road to travel and the biggest obstacles to overcome. Of all the characters, he changed the most since the beginning of the series. He made a lot of mistakes and bad choices along the way, but in the end he had the

courage and honor to stand up to his father and help Aang defeat him.

BRYAN: Physically and bending—wise, I'd say Toph is probably the toughest of the bunch. Aang is probably the most spiritually strong, and Katara probably has the strongest heart. Sokka definitely has the strongest appetite, and I can relate to that kind of strength.

Is Azula really as evil as she seems? Or is there more to her?

MIKE: As with all the AVATAR characters, even Azula has a softer side, though it's buried very deep. As "The Beach" and "Sozin's Comet" showed, she has a lot of unresolved issues with her mother. She really feels that her mother didn't love her as much as Zuko, and this drives her crazy, literally.

BRYAN: There are obviously some truly evil people in the world, but in the case of Azula, her repressed emotions and jealousies corroded her spirit and made her become that way. It is possible that she could have turned out better in a healthier environment, but growing up in the royal family of a nation seeking world domination proved to exacerbate her problems. But Zuko and Katara spared her life, and who knows, she might have a chance to heal.

What's next for the world of AVATAR, now that the Fire Lord has finally been defeated and peace has been restored? We all know there's talk of a movie—will you two play a major role in its plot?

MIKE: We have some ideas to further expand the AVATAR world, but it's in the very early stages right now. We're keeping busy by finishing up the last few episodes and serving as executive producers of the AVATAR live—action movie. The movie is an adaptation of Book 1: Water, which M. Night Shyamalan is writing, producing, and directing. We're having a great time working with him to make the movie something really special.